Dance with Angelina

A Sticker Storybook

Illustrations by Helen Craig
Based on the text by Katharine Holabird

Published by Pleasant Company Publications.
© 2000 Helen Craig Limited and Katharine Holabird.

Edited by Michelle Jones and Yvette La Pierre
Art Directed and Designed by Justin Packard and Lynne Wells
Cover Spot Illustrations by Judy Pelikan

The Angelina Ballerina name and character and the dancing Angelina logo are trademarks of
HIT Entertainment PLC, Katharine Holabird, and Helen Craig. ANGELINA is registered
in the U.K. and Japan. The dancing Angelina logo is registered in the U.K.

Visit our Web sites at **www.americangirl.com** and
Angelina's very own site at **www.angelinaballerina.com**

Printed in China
First Edition
04 05 06 07 08 09 10 C&C 14 13 12 11 10 9 8

Angelina loves to dance. She dances everywhere—
even in her dreams. Find two Angelinas in pink tutus
to complete Angelina's dream.

Angelina is doing an arabesque in the kitchen.
Oops! She knocked over the Cheddar cheese pies!
Find Angelina with her leg raised high behind her.

Every day after school Angelina hurries to ballet class
with her ballet dress and slippers. Find Angelina carrying
her ballet bag.

At ballet class, Angelina and the other girls practice curtsies and pliés. Find three ballerinas in tutus Angelina can practice with.

In gym class, Angelina is learning to dance with a ribbon.
Find Angelina in her pink gym dress and Alice in her
green gym dress.

In winter, Angelina dances on the ice. Find Angelina in her red skates. Find her some friends to practice spins and turns with.

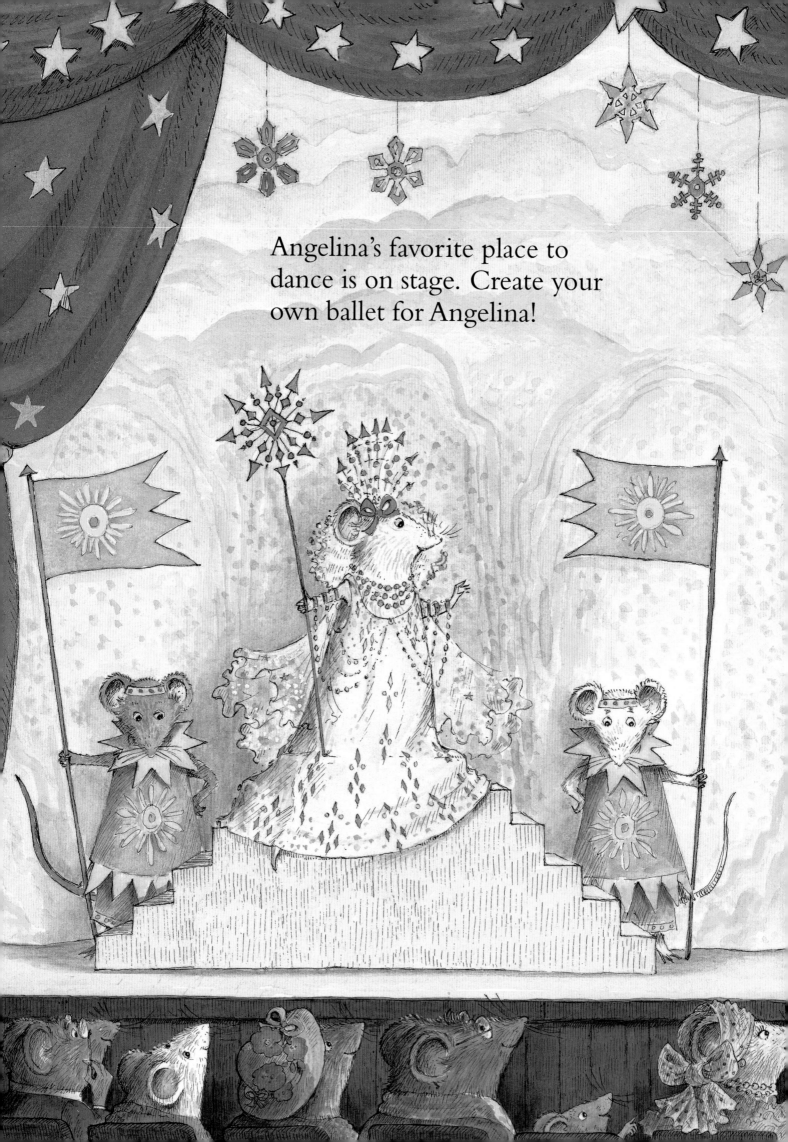

Angelina's favorite place to dance is on stage. Create your own ballet for Angelina!